SHERRI DUSKEY RINKER AND AG FORD

Construction Site:

Road Crew, Coming Through!

chronicle books · san francisco

Six mighty friends are on their way
to help with something BIG today.
They're off to work on something new . . .

to join the big ROAD-BUILDING crew!
(There's a GIANT job to do!)

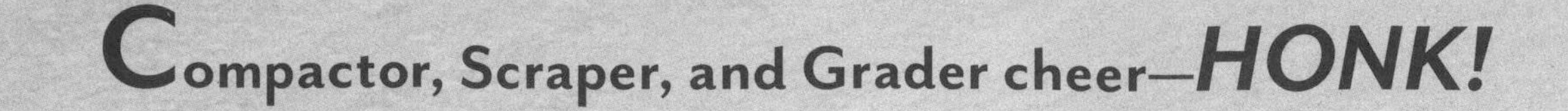

Compactor, Scraper, and Grader cheer—***HONK!***

Roller and Striper get into gear. ***VROOM!***

Water Truck is set to go,

and Paver's pipes both snort and blow! ***HUFF!***

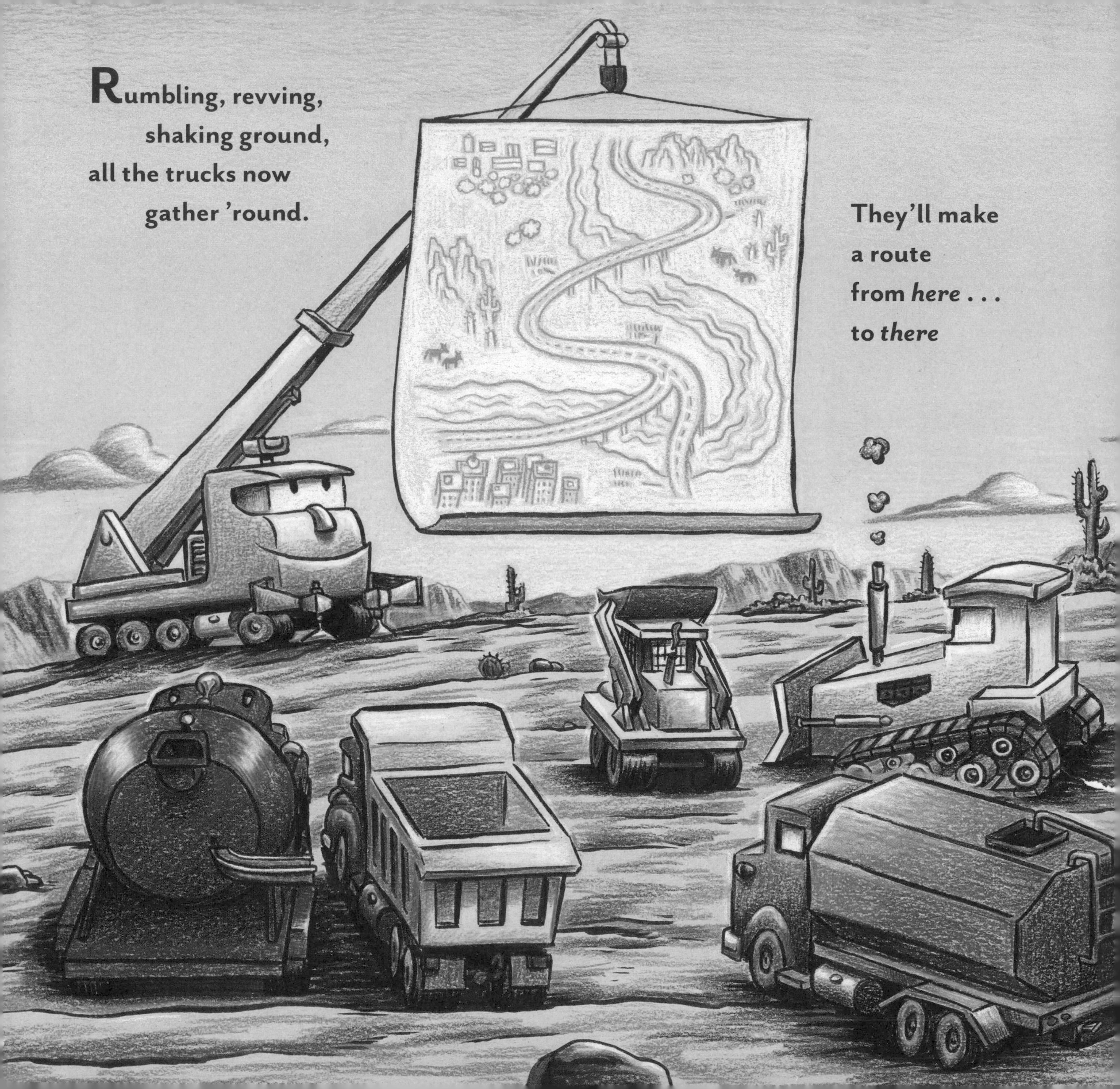

Rumbling, revving,
shaking ground,
all the trucks now
gather 'round.

They'll make
a route
from *here* . . .
to *there*

with careful planning, thought, and care.
The team will build it, load by load:

A SUPERHIGHWAY, MEGA ROAD!

Excavator, to begin,
gets to work by digging in.
Scooping heavy loads with ease,
he lifts out boulders,
trash, and trees.

Skid Steer's doing her part, too,
and in no time at all—
they're through!

They clear tons of loads today—
and Dump Truck hauls them all away.

Big Bulldozer rolls on-site,
pushing through with
all his might.

Clearing stumps and rocks
and rubble,
ripping, tearing, without trouble.

Then sturdy Scraper is at hand
to move the earth and reshape land.
With care and speed, she rolls along,
cutting, clearing—smooth and strong.

With her sharp and rugged blade,
the embankment and roadbed are made.

When the grit begins to fly,
Water Truck is standing by.
Her jets squirt water on the ground,
so dust and dirt won't blow around.
She's keeping the air clear today,
so all the trucks can see their way.

Compactor has the job he likes,
rolling, squishing, with his spikes.

His heavy wheels push down hard—
smashing, mashing, yard by yard.

Now Grader knows just what to do:
her blade will easily cut through—
leveling each bump and groove,
she leaves the surface flat and smooth.

Her hopper's filled—

now Paver's ready!

Slowly rolling, strong and steady,
her screed arm lays the asphalt down—
a strong new layer on the ground.
Spreading blacktop all the way,
she'll cover this whole road today!

Roller's 22-ton load
goes over every inch of road.
Back and forth, until he's done,
he smashes down on every ton.

Pushing! Squishing! And just like *that*,
he makes the surface hard and flat.

Now, a bridge—an overpass—
needs strong concrete so it will last.
Cement Mixer drives onto the scene,
pouring each load, smooth and clean.

Then he starts the curb and gutter.
He churns and pours without a sputter,
lining both sides of the street
with miles and miles of fresh concrete.

Crane Truck hangs the signs and lights,
and sets them in, all straight and tight.

He holds them firmly—
they won't sway
on this very windy day.

And now, before the work's complete,
Striper Truck will mark the street.

Ribbons sprayed on, clean and bright:

some are yellow, some are white.

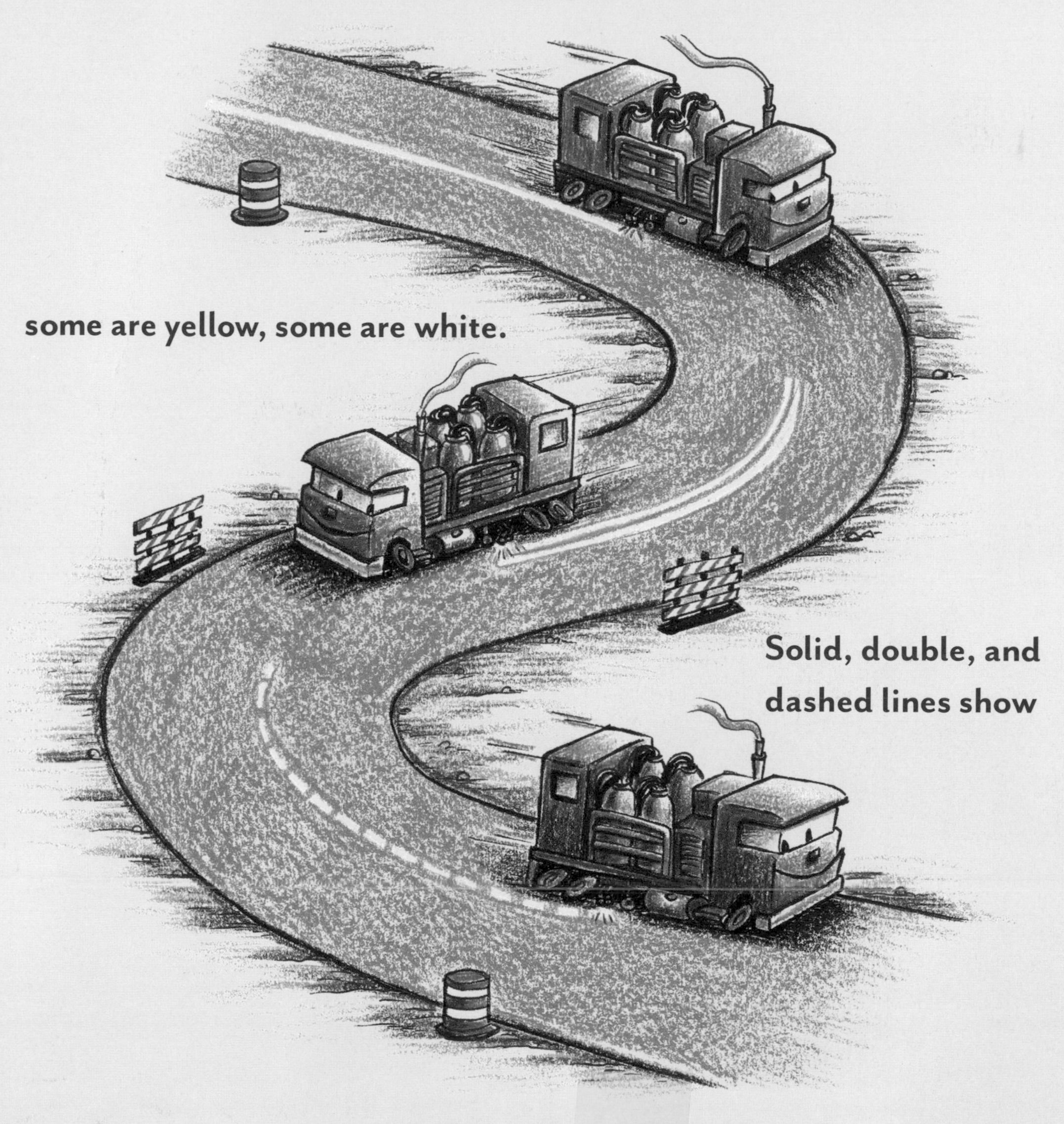

Solid, double, and
dashed lines show

all the traffic where to go.

There's just one more thing to do:
let the traffic all drive through!
The road is opened up, at last,
and all the cars go swooshing past!

Everyone is on their way—
heading home to end their day.

The trucks turn back to look, and smile:

"This was AWESOME—every mile!"

This great big job was tough—but fun!
And now they drive off, one by one,
proud that they have done their best.
The trucks roll home to get some rest.

Away they rumble, out of sight.
Good job, road builders . . .

and, *goodnight*.

Did you notice the coyote walking along the river, under the bridge? Animals need paths for traveling, too! More and more, road builders are thinking about these travelers and how we can best share our great big world with them. Sometimes this means specially planted bridges across a freeway so that elk can migrate in safety. Sometimes it means special tunnels under a road so that salamanders can find their ponds. And sometimes it just means making sure there's some extra space around waterways. These wildlife crossings can be found around the world, helping to make passages for the many lives around us. Creatures as diverse as mountain goats, Florida panthers, desert tortoises, crabs, penguins, and squirrel gliders all benefit from these crossings, which help everyone to get home safely.

For my brother, Mike Zdenek, with gratitude for all of your expertise and support. And for Hannah Zdenek, my awesome and amazing niece —S. D. R.

To my sons, Maddox and Carter —A. F.

Library of Congress Cataloging-in-Publication Data available.

ISBN 978-1-7972-0472-7

Manufactured in China.

Design by Jennifer Tolo Pierce.
Typeset in Mr. Eaves San OT.
The illustrations in this book were rendered in Neocolor wax oil crayons.

10 9 8 7 6 5 4 3 2 1

Chronicle books and gifts are available at special quantity discounts to corporations, professional associations, literacy programs, and other organizations. For details and discount information, please contact our premiums department at corporatesales@chroniclebooks.com or at 1-800-759-0190.

Chronicle Books LLC
680 Second Street
San Francisco, California 94107

Chronicle Books—we see things differently.
Become part of our community at www.chroniclekids.com.